At the Side of
MOSES

At the Side of
MOSES

A Multiple-Ending
Bible Adventure

Written by
Eric Pakulak

Illustrated by
David Fielding

BOOKS & MEDIA

Boston

Library of Congress Cataloging-in-Publication Data

Pakulak, Eric.
    At the side of Moses : a multiple-ending Bible adventure /
written by Eric Pakulak ; illustrated by David Fielding.
        p. cm.
    Summary : As the fictional friend of Moses, the reader
makes decisions about the outcome of various episodes in
Moses' life as recorded in the Old Testament, with different
plot developments depending on the choices.
    ISBN 0-8198-0770-2 (pbk.)
    1. Moses (Biblical leader)—Juvenile fiction. 2. Plot-your-
own stories. [1. Moses (Biblical leader) 2. Plot-your-own
stories.] I. Fielding, David, 1946– ill. II. Title.
    PZ7.P174 Au 2000
    [Fic]—dc21

                                                    00-010186

Printed and published in the U.S.A. by Pauline Books & Media,
50 Saint Pauls Avenue, Boston, MA 02130-3491.

www.pauline.org

Pauline Books & Media is the publishing house of the Daughters
of St. Paul, an international congregation of women religious
serving the Church with the communications media.

1 2 3 4 5 6   05 04 03 02 01 00

For Mom and Dad,
whose love and support
mean more than words
can express

About This Book...

At the Side of Moses is based on the Bible's story of Moses, the man chosen by God to lead the Israelites from slavery in Egypt to freedom in the Promised Land.

As you read, you will enter into the action as Moses' *imaginary* friend. You'll even have your own decisions to make.

The author and the publisher hope that interacting with this Bible story will help you to think about the values that formed Moses into one of the greatest heroes of the Jewish people.

A slight wind chills you as you make your way up the mountain trail, holding on to the rocks on either side for balance. Just ahead of you is your friend Moses, patiently searching under every clump of underbrush for two lambs that have wandered away. Although you're very tired from a long day of tending sheep in the meadow below, you must help Moses find them.

"Come here, little one," you hear Moses saying. You look up to see that he's found one of the strays. "Take our friend back down to his brothers," he tells you as he hands you the lamb. "I'll keep searching for the second one."

As you backtrack down the trail, the rays of the late afternoon sun warm your face. You think about Moses. Just as the sun brings needed comfort, so has Moses' friendship comforted you in this land of Midian, so far from your homeland of Canaan.

You'll never forget the day when, after a long journey through the desert, you met Moses in the fields. It was almost as if God had sent him to you.

Moses somehow sensed that you were, like him, an Israelite in a foreign land. He had put a welcoming arm around you. You soon became best friends, and his wisdom helped you adjust to your new life as a shepherd of the flock of Jethro, the priest of Midian.

In a short time you reach the bottom of the mountain. As the little lamb happily runs off to join the others in the meadow, you sit to rest on a flat rock. After a few minutes you glance back up the trail. Moses is still nowhere to be seen. You start to worry, but you catch yourself. *He'll be fine,* you think. *After all, he's faced much greater dangers in his life....*

Moses has told you the incredible story of his early life. He was born during a terrible time in Egypt, a time when Pharaoh commanded that all baby Israelite boys be put to death. Moses' mother hid him for three months. When she couldn't hide him any longer, she put him into a small cradle-boat and placed it carefully in the river by the bank. Moses' sister Miriam kept watch nearby. Soon Pharaoh's daughter came to the river to bathe. She found the little boat and took pity on the Israelite baby. That's when Miriam came forward and offered to find an Israelite woman to nurse him. When

the princess agreed, Miriam went and got her own mother. The princess allowed her to take Moses home and care for him.

When he was old enough, Moses was adopted by the princess and brought to the palace to live. While living the wonderful life of an Egyptian prince at the palace, he also had to watch the horrible suffering of his people. The Israelites were slaves in Egypt. They were forced to work long hours in the burning sun and were treated cruelly by their harsh guards. Once when Moses was already a grown man, he saw an Egyptian guard beating an Israelite worker. Moses grew so angry, he killed the guard. He thought no one had seen, and he buried the guard in the sand. But soon Moses discovered that the Egyptians—including Pharaoh—had found out about the incident and wanted to kill *him!*

Moses escaped from Egypt to Midian. There, one day, he saw shepherds trying to drive some young women away from the well. Moses helped them to stand up for their rights. These young women were the daughters of Jethro, and Moses ended up living with Jethro's family. He married Jethro's daughter Zipporah, and took charge of the family's flock of sheep. That's when you met him—after he had settled into the rugged life of a shepherd. Soon the two of you were herding flocks together and climbing the rocky trail up Mount Sinai in search of stray sheep.

Suddenly your thoughts of the past are interrupted by the sound of footsteps. You turn to see Moses approaching. As he comes closer, you notice that he has a very strange expression on his face. He looks stunned, as though he has just seen something incredible. Without saying a word, he sits down beside you.

"Moses, what happened?" you ask. "Are you all right?"

"Yes, my friend," he says in a whisper. "God has just spoken to me."

You take a deep breath and start to answer him, but you're left speechless by this amazing news. God, the one true God of your people, has chosen Moses and spoken to him!

"God is ready to bring our people out of their suffering in Egypt and into the Promised Land," Moses tells you. "He's chosen me to be his messenger to Pharaoh. I must get ready to leave for Egypt immediately." Moses' eyes meet yours. "I'd like you to come with me. It will be a long and possibly dangerous journey." Moses pauses and looks at the ground. "I understand if you'd rather stay here."

For a moment you're shocked and confused. Everything is happening so quickly! You're happy with your life in Midian. Are you really ready to risk a dangerous journey to a distant land where your people are held as slaves? You remember the support Moses gave you when you first arrived in Midian. *It would only be right to support him now,* you think.

If you stay in Midian, turn to page 13.

If you go with Moses to Egypt, turn to page 26.

"My prayers will be with you," you promise Moses, "but I think I'd be better off staying here."

"I understand," he answers. "Besides, someone has to take good care of our sheep."

You smile, happy that your friend is so accepting, and turn your attention back to the sheep. The two of you guide the flock back home, where Moses tells Jethro of his amazing encounter.

"You will be missed," says Jethro as he embraces Moses, "but I wish you happiness."

The next day you're very busy helping Moses prepare for his journey. You want to ask him more about his conversation with God, but there's too much to do and just not enough time. As you help Moses pack, you wonder about the adventure that lies ahead of him.

Soon your friend is ready to leave, and you send him off with a hearty embrace. As his wagons head off beneath the desert sun, you hope it isn't the last time you'll see Moses. And you wonder if you've made the right choice.

The next few months are lonely ones as you continue watching the sheep in the fields. You can't help remembering the long talks you used to have with your good friend. Now you have only your thoughts to keep you company. You spend peaceful evenings talking with Jethro and other friends, but there's still something missing in your life.

As the months go by, you grow accustomed to life in Midian without Moses, although you continue to think of him every day as you watch the sheep. One day, after you've brought the flock in for the night, Jethro frantically runs up to you.

"A messenger came through today with news of Moses!" he exclaims. "He's led the Israelites out of Egypt, but Pharaoh and the Egyptians are pursuing them even as we speak!"

Your first impulse is to try to find Moses and help him in any way you can. But this could mean risking your life.

If you set off to try to find Moses, turn to page 22.

If you stay in Midian, turn to page 15.

14

As much as you want to help Moses, you're afraid to put yourself at risk. You say a special prayer for him and go on with your life in Midian.

The long, hot days are even lonelier as you think of Moses and the danger he faces from the Egyptians. At the end of every day, you rush to Jethro with the hope that there is some news. And every day he slowly shakes his head, looks down at the ground, and says the same thing: "I'm sorry, my son, but there is no news of Moses today."

Finally, after several months, word of your friend does arrive. Jethro rushes out to meet you as you bring in the flock. "Moses has escaped the Egyptians and is camped nearby! I'm going to see him. Would you like to come?"

"Yes!" you practically shout.

The next day you and Jethro set out at the first streak of dawn. After a short journey across the desert, you reach the edge of the wilderness surrounding Mount Sinai, the place where God first spoke to Moses. You struggle through some thick underbrush, and when you come to the clearing you're amazed. There are people and livestock camped everywhere, as far as your eyes can see. Their robes, once bright white, are now stained by months of exposure to sun and sand. While most of the people sit slumped against rocks or trees in exhaustion, there is still a gleam in their eyes that convinces you that they are taking part in something truly miraculous. As you squeeze through the crowd, several men approach you and block your way.

"Who are you and what do you want?" says one.

"I am the father-in-law of Moses," explains Jethro, "and this is one of his very good friends from Midian."

"In that case, welcome," replies the man, his stern look turning to a smile. "Follow me."

He leads you to the base of the mountain, and as you approach the opening of a small cave, you see Moses speaking to a group of men. When he turns toward you, you see how tired and worn his face looks. Still, at the sight of you and Jethro his eyes light up and a smile spreads across his weary face. He rushes up to you.

"I'm so happy you're safe!" you cry.

"The Lord is with us," replies Moses.

He invites the two of you to sit down. Then he begins an incredible story. Moses tells you how God was forced to inflict ten plagues on Egypt before Pharaoh would let the Israelites go. He describes how God led them through the desert by a cloud during the day and a pillar of fire during the night as the Egyptians chased them. Moses even tells you how God gave him the power to separate the waters of the Red Sea to allow the Israelites to escape the Egyptians!

"Now I know your God is greater than all other gods!" cries Jethro, who is not even an Israelite. With that, Moses' brother Aaron and some elders join you, offering you something to eat and drink.

"I'm sorry, my friends," Moses says after a few minutes, "but I must get back to the people."

He stands and returns to the edge of the wilderness, where the group of people waiting for him has grown. You and Jethro watch for hours as Moses answers questions and settles disputes among the Israelites in the name of God. When Moses finally returns, Jethro shakes his head.

"You'll surely wear yourself out," he tells him. "You must teach others to judge and provide counsel to the people, so that the burden is not all on you."

Moses thanks Jethro for the advice and immediately sets off to seek out men to serve as counselors. Then Jethro turns to you.

"I will now return to Midian," he says. "This is not a journey for me. If you would like to say farewell to Moses and come back to live with me, you are most welcome. But I understand if you want to join Moses on the journey to the land your God has promised you."

If you return to Midian with Jethro, turn to page 19.

If you stay with Moses and journey to the Promised Land, turn to page 21.

"I'd like to return with you to Midian," you answer Jethro. When Moses comes back, you take him aside and tell him of your decision.

"Of course I'm disappointed that you won't be at my side for the journey to the land God is giving us," he says quietly. "But you must do what is best for you. I wish you a long and prosperous life, my friend."

You embrace Moses and wipe tears from your eyes as you turn to leave. Walking past the thousands of people in the Israelite camp, you think of the joy they'll feel upon reaching their new homeland. You wonder if you're making the right decision. You put this thought out of your mind and continue on your way with Jethro. Soon you find yourself back in Midian.

It's not long before you've settled back into your daily routine of watching Jethro's flock. Although the work is sometimes difficult and lonely, you enjoy it and gradually make new friends as Jethro hires more shepherds. You still think of Moses from time to time. Then one day a few sheep wander up the rocky slope of a mountain. You sense that the place is very familiar and that you've been here before—you and Moses. You sit on a rock and look out over the horizon. And you wonder whatever happened to your friend Moses...

The End

"I appreciate your offer," you tell Jethro, "but I now know that my place is here with Moses and my people."

"Very well," he says as he warmly clasps your hands. "I wish you good fortune on your journey."

Jethro then says good-bye to Moses and heads back to Midian.

Turn to page 78.

You realize that you must go to be with Moses during this difficult time, and you explain this to Jethro.

"I understand," he replies, "even though I hate to lose a good shepherd."

With Jethro's help you gather some things for the journey, and at dawn you set off.

Traveling through the desert for several long days, you begin to wonder if you ever *will* find Moses. One evening, as you stop to drink at a small stream, a group of men approaches from the opposite direction. You ask them if they have any word of the Israelites coming from Egypt.

"Oh yes! What a horrible situation!" says one as he shakes his head. "The poor Israelites are quickly approaching the Red Sea. They'll be trapped when the Egyptians catch up to them."

When the travelers explain that the Red Sea is nearby, you speed off in that direction. Soon you come to a bluff. An astonishing scene lies before you. Immediately below surge the deep waters of the Red Sea, with rough winds kicking up great white-capped waves as far as you can see. On one side of the water, you see a mass of people and livestock that seems larger than the sea itself! In front of the crowd is a huge dark cloud the likes of which you've never seen before. It rises from the ground up to the sky like a giant pillar. And there, stretching across the horizon, is a line of chariots gleaming in the fading light. It's the approaching Egyptian army! Your heart begins to pound. You realize that there's nothing you can do to save Moses and your people from this desperate situation.

The gigantic crowd seems to be moving toward one point along the shore. As you look closer, you see the silhouette of a man with arms outstretched over the water. It must be Moses! Just as you're trying to figure out what he's doing, you witness the most amazing event of your life…. The powerful wind suddenly picks up and the waters of the Red Sea begin to separate to form a passageway through the middle of the water! As you continue your watch during the night, the Israelites march straight through the parted walls of water. You look on in wonder as the last Israelite reaches the shore below you. At that point the Egyptian army catches up and storms into the passageway in chase. As the thundering army comes closer, you wonder if the Israelites will be able to escape. Just then, Moses returns to the edge of the sea. He raises his arms again and suddenly the water comes crashing down on the entire Egyptian army! The Israelites are saved!

You rush down the bluff in search of your friend Moses. It takes you a long time to reach the Israelites, but they're still celebrating when you finally get there. You make your way through groups of singing and dancing people until you reach the shoreline. There you find what appears to be a gathering of Israelite elders. As you approach them, a guard steps in your way. But Moses happens to glance over and see you. He signals the guard to let you through.

"How wonderful to see you!" he shouts as he embraces you and introduces you to his brother Aaron and the other elders.

"I'd like to join you for the rest of the journey to the Promised Land," you tell Moses.

"Of course," he says. "It will be long and difficult, but I'll be happy to have you with me."

Turn to page 60.

"Of course I'll come with you," you tell Moses. "This is very important for you and our people. I want to be at your side."

"Thank you, my friend," he replies. "Come now, we must give Jethro the news and prepare for the journey."

Jethro is left speechless for a moment, but then he wishes you the best on your journey. You and Moses quickly gather some belongings, load them onto several donkeys, and set off.

The trip to Egypt is treacherous, since it requires traveling through the desert and wilderness. But the thought that God has chosen your friend Moses for a special mission keeps you going. As you travel, Moses relates more about his encounter with God on the mountain. He tells you about how God called to him from a burning bush that was not consumed by the fire. He tells you how surprised he was that God had chosen him. He explains that he asked the Lord how he was supposed to convince the Israelites that God had really appeared to him. God then showed him signs to prove that it was true. "God told me to throw my staff to the ground. Then he turned it into a snake! I was so frightened, I jumped," Moses admits with a chuckle.

"But then God had me take it by the tail, and when I did, it turned back into a staff!"

Moses also tells you how God made his hand turn white and withered, then changed it back to normal again.

"He told me to show these signs to the Israelites," Moses says, "so that they will believe me."

"Were you nervous about what God was asking you to do?" you ask Moses.

"Yes, I was," he replies. "I told God that I don't speak well enough to go before the people. But God said that I should bring my brother Aaron with me, because *he* is a good speaker. We'll meet Aaron at Mount Sinai, that mountain up ahead."

You see the rocky face of a mountain rising from the desert before you, and soon you're approaching the area at its base. A smiling man comes rushing toward you.

"My brother!" shouts Moses as he runs to Aaron. "It's so wonderful to see you!"

Moses introduces you to Aaron, and soon the three of you are back on the road to Egypt, with Moses telling his brother of his conversation with God. Time passes quickly. Before you know it, you're looking out over a vast plain. A huge river is branching off into the sea like fingers from a hand. It's the mighty Nile, and you're in Egypt.

You journey down into the valley and soon come across some Israelites hard at work in a field. Moses approaches a few of the older workers, speaks with them briefly, then returns to you and Aaron as the men rush off through the fields.

"They've gone to gather the Israelite elders," Moses informs you. "We'll speak to them, and they'll tell the people about us."

Soon you stand watching as Moses describes his mission to lead the Israelites out of Egypt to a group of old, wise-looking men. They listen intently with furrowed brows. After Moses has explained everything, he takes his staff and throws it to the ground. The elders jump back, eyes wide with fear, as the staff suddenly turns into a huge, hissing snake. It moves closer as if to strike. But before that can happen, Moses seizes it by the tail, and right before your eyes it turns back into the staff. As the still wide-eyed old men continue to watch, Moses puts his hand into his robe. When he pulls it out, it's ghostly white and covered with wrinkles and blisters! The elders gasp in horror. Moses puts his hand back into his tunic. When he takes it out a second time, it's completely normal again. You've never seen such miracles in your life!

The elders are also amazed, and they quickly bow down before Moses. "We are so thankful that God is aware of our suffering and has sent someone to lead us back home," they tell him.

As the elders leave to bring word of Moses' arrival to the Israelites in Egypt, Moses turns to you.

"It's now time for Aaron and I to go speak with Pharaoh," he says. "If you would like to come with us for support, I would welcome you. Otherwise you can wait for us here."

If you go with Moses and Aaron to see Pharaoh, turn to page 35.

If you stay in the fields with the Israelites, turn to page 30.

"I'd like to stay here for now," you tell Moses. "But I'll be with you in spirit."

"I know you will, my friend," he replies, smiling and resting his hand on your shoulder.

Early the next morning you see Moses and Aaron off, then sit down to breakfast with some of the men and women of the camp where you're staying. Before you're able to eat a single bite, however, five large Egyptian soldiers with spears storm into the camp.

"It's time to get to work!" they shout. As you stare at them in disbelief, one of the soldiers hits you with the handle of his spear. "Didn't you hear me?!"

You jump up and follow the others out into the fields. In minutes you're hard at work beneath the blazing morning sun. After only a few hours your muscles burn with pain. For the first time you understand just how difficult slave life has been for the Israelites.

"I don't know how much more of this I can take," says one man at a mid-morning water break.

"You won't have to suffer much longer," you say, "because Moses has come to lead you back to your homeland."

"Are you mad?" the man replies. "Your friend Moses will only make life harder for us by getting Pharaoh angry!"

"Yes," agrees another man. "We've been talking about trying to escape. Now's the time, before Pharaoh decides to double our workload."

"And you, friend," says one of the men to you, "will suffer more than anyone, for you're a companion of this Moses. Come with us now, before it's too late."

These remarks make you think. Maybe it would be wise to try to escape, just in case Moses isn't successful with Pharaoh. But Moses is your friend, and God has sent him on this mission. It might be best to wait and see what happens....

If you try to escape with the men, turn to page 32.

If you remain with the Israelites, turn to page 33.

"Maybe you're right," you tell the men. "Let's go!"

As everyone returns to work, you follow the men to the edge of the field. They're carefully watching the guard, and when he turns his back for a moment they grab your arm. "Now! Quickly!"

You run as fast as you can, following the men across a nearby road and into a ditch on the far side of the field. You crawl through the ditch, past all of the fields on the opposite side, until you finally reach one of the main roads leading out of Egypt. Just when you begin to think you're out of danger, someone behind you shouts, "Halt!"

You turn to see several guards rushing toward you. You break into a run, but the guards are gaining on you. Suddenly arrows begin whizzing past your head. One of the men next to you falls. You keep running, but it looks hopeless. You wish you could run faster. You also wish you had had more faith in God...and in Moses...

The End

"Thank you for the offer," you tell the men, "but my place is with Moses, and I have faith that he will do the work of God and lead us to freedom."

"As you wish," one of them answers.

Thoughts of Moses and your prayers to God bring you new strength and courage as you head back to work in the fields. Your muscles continue to ache, but now it doesn't matter. You're able to get through the day. You have supper with the other workers and wait for word of Moses, who must still be at Pharaoh's palace.

After your meal, an Israelite man comes running into the camp. "I have news," he says breathlessly. "Pharaoh has laughed at Moses and our one true God. Now he's sure to try to kill us all with more work!"

The man explains that Pharaoh has ordered his soldiers not to supply straw to the Israelite slaves who make mud bricks. This means that the slaves will have to gather their own straw while still being expected to make as many bricks as before.

"That's impossible!" several people cry.

The messenger grimly adds that those Israelites who work in the fields will also be made to work twice as hard or face beatings from the guards.

It's not long before you find this out for yourself. Before sunrise the next morning, Egyptian soldiers pull you out of bed and force you into the fields with the other workers. You're exhausted, and you're still sore from the previous day's work, but you again find strength in your faith. You're determined to do your part to fight Pharaoh, just as Moses is doing his part.

The Egyptian soldiers work you so hard in the desert heat that you're barely able to stand by the end of the day. When the messenger from the city arrives, he tells how unimpressed Pharaoh was with the miracles Moses performed. The people around you sigh in disappointment. You think of Moses and realize that you want to be with him to offer your encouragement. As the messenger turns to leave, you ask him to show you the way into the city and to bring you to Moses.

"Come," he says.

Wishing the Israelites well, you tell them to continue to have faith in Moses. Then you set off with the messenger. It's not long before you're standing in the shadow of Pharaoh's great palace and, seeing Moses, you rush over to him.

"It's good to have you here," he says.

Turn to page 41.

"Yes, I'd like to come," you reply.

"I'm glad," Moses answers with a smile.

At dawn, you set off with Moses and Aaron. Several Israelite elders show you the way through the fields and into the city. You soon find yourself standing in front of a building so big that it reminds you of some of the mountains of Midian. It's Pharaoh's palace! The elders have arranged for a meeting, and two palace guards appear to lead you inside. After going through a maze of corridors, you're led into a long hall supported by huge wooden pillars. The pillars form a walkway leading to the far end of the room where a man sits on a throne of gold. As you approach, you see that he is wearing the royal headdress adorned with a golden cobra at the center of the forehead, and a breastplate of pure gold. His dark eyes blaze with intensity as he stares at your group.

"What do you want?" he says slowly, his deep voice echoing throughout the hall. "Speak."

Moses and Aaron step forward. "The Lord God of Israel asks that you let his people go to the wilderness to worship."

Pharaoh looks puzzled for a moment then laughs out loud. "And who is this God of the Israelites? I do not know this God, and I will not let the Israelites go."

Moses and Aaron ask again, but Pharaoh again refuses and begins to get angry. "Your talk of this God takes the people away from their work. Because of this I shall see to it that they work even harder!"

He calls in a guard and commands that the Israelites no longer be given the straw they need to make bricks. "But they must make the same amount of bricks as before," he declares, "or they shall be beaten."

You follow as Moses and Aaron slowly walk away, heads hung low. You think about how powerful Pharaoh is and wonder if the situation is hopeless. You consider offering to work for the Egyptians before you're punished along with Moses and Aaron. *But,* you think, *Moses is my friend, and he really needs my support at a time like this. Maybe I should have more faith and believe that God will show Moses how to overcome Pharaoh.*

If you try to go work for the Egyptians, turn to page 38.

If you stay with Moses, turn to page 40.

Although you feel bad about leaving your friend, you reason that you must also look out for your own safety. You spend the night with Moses and Aaron at an Israelite camp in the city. But you wake up before the others and slip away in the darkness of the early morning.

As you approach the palace, a guard stops you. "What do you want here?" he demands.

"I've come to offer my services," you reply.

"Aren't you one of the Israelites?" he asks.

"No, no," you say. You feel bad about lying, but you don't want to be punished.

The guard leads you to speak with a representative of Pharaoh, and soon you're given work on the outskirts of the city. Ironically, your assignment is to help the Egyptian guards oversee the Israelites who are making bricks. Although it hurts you to watch your people being beaten, you're relieved to be alive and free.

As the weeks go by, you hear that Moses is battling against Pharaoh with strange plagues sent by God. At first you wonder what this means. You find out soon enough....

One morning you hear a faint hum in the distance. It gradually becomes a roaring buzz. Suddenly there are flies everywhere. They blind your eyes, swarming over your face, head, and entire body. Wherever you go there are flies! Just when you feel you can stand them no longer, the flies disappear. A few days later your arm begins to itch. You're shocked to discover that it's covered with large red boils! Soon your whole body is covered with these same sores, and it hurts even to move. The Egyptian guards are also afflicted with boils, but none of the Israelites are. You begin to wonder if it was a mistake to leave Moses. As you sit in pain thinking about this, hail the size of stones begins to fall from the sky. You try to find shelter, but there's no time. There's only time for you to understand that it was a mistake to leave your friend…

The End

Although it's a difficult situation, you know there is no way you will leave Moses to go to work for the Egyptians.

After a restless night at an Israelite camp in the city, and a long day thinking of the unsuccessful meeting with Pharaoh, you find yourself standing with Moses and Aaron outside the palace.

Turn to page 41.

A group of Israelites is just coming out of the palace. When they see Moses, they approach you.

"You came to save us," accuses one man angrily, "but you've only made our life worse! Pharaoh will now work us twice as hard as before!"

Moses winces with pain at these harsh words. "I must talk with the Lord," he whispers as he leaves. You want to follow him, but Aaron gently holds you back. It's hours before Moses returns, but when he does you can see that he feels better.

"God has given me guidance," he says. "We must show Pharaoh the Lord's power."

The next day Moses awakens you before dawn. Sunrise finds you waiting outside Pharaoh's palace with Moses and Aaron. You're finally admitted into the ruler's presence. He laughs when you enter the room.

"Have you come again to speak of your God?" he asks mockingly. "If he is the one true God, let him show me his power."

Aaron steps forward with his staff in hand. He throws the staff down in front of Pharaoh, and as soon as it hits the floor, it turns into a large black snake. The snake hisses at Pharaoh and coils up before him.

Pharaoh becomes nervous. You wonder if he will let the Israelites go now.

"Guard!" he shouts. "Summon my sorcerers!"

A few minutes later, several men wearing dark robes and carrying tall staffs enter the room. You watch in disbelief as the sorcerers, each in turn, throw down their staffs, which instantly become snakes— bigger than the one produced from Aaron's staff! The sorcerers' snakes slither menacingly toward Aaron's snake. All at once, the snake from Aaron's staff, with its jaws wide open, swallows *all* of the other snakes! *Surely Pharaoh will let the Israelites go now,* you think. But you're wrong.

"Leave me!" Pharaoh commands.

You follow Moses and Aaron out of the palace in silence. Again, Moses goes off by himself to speak with God. Returning late that evening, he says nothing to you. The next morning, you and Aaron accompany Moses to the river. Pharaoh and his servants are resting on the bank. Moses approaches them.

"Raise your staff and strike the waters," Moses orders Aaron.

Aaron plunges his staff into the water and it suddenly turns to blood! A terrible odor rises from the river as dead fish begin to surface everywhere.

Without saying a word, Pharaoh turns abruptly and walks back toward the palace.

Over the course of the next week, the subject of Pharaoh's stubbornness comes up in many of your conversations with Moses. Moses reminds you of the power of your one true God, and tells you to have faith. "The Lord has many miracles in store for Pharaoh," he says.

Before long, you again find yourself with Moses and Aaron at the river as Pharaoh approaches. Aaron steps forward and waves his staff over the water. A few frogs immediately jump onto the shore. But in a short time, you're surrounded by hundreds of them! They're everywhere now—in the city streets, in the grain carts, even in the Egyptians' houses. Pharaoh begins to walk away in silence, but he goes only a few feet before he turns toward Moses in anger.

"Very well!" he shouts. "Get rid of these frogs and I will let your people go!"

With that, Moses rushes off to speak with the Lord, and soon all the frogs begin to die. The Egyptians bring buckets full of dead frogs from their homes and make piles in the streets. The whole city is filled with such a stench that you can hardly breathe. You imagine how wonderful it will be to get away from all this. Just then, Pharaoh comes out of his palace. "I've changed my mind," he calls to Moses. "I won't let the Israelites go!"

Moses moves toward you and you know from the expression on his face that he is as determined as ever. You remember what he said about the power of God and the miracles God has in store for Pharaoh.

Over the next few months, more miraculous things happen. God sends swarms of gnats that bite only the Egyptians, not touching the Israelites. Then millions of flies descend upon the city, creating a buzz that hums through the streets day and night. Pharaoh again agrees to let the Israelites go and then changes his mind, so the Lord brings illness upon Egypt. First comes a disease that kills many of the Egyptians' cattle. This is followed by a sickness that affects the Egyptians themselves. Before long, all the Egyptians are so weak they can barely walk the streets, and their bodies are covered with painful red boils. Even with his people suffering so terribly, Pharaoh still refuses to release the Israelites.

God then sends a great hailstorm over Egypt. Hailstones as big as rocks destroy most of the Egyptians' crops. Right after the hailstorm, a great wind blows in from the east bringing swarms of locusts that eat the few remaining crops. Again,

Pharaoh stubbornly refuses to give in, so the Lord brings forth a darkness so deep that the Egyptians can't even see inside their houses. Amazingly, during this darkness, which lasts for three whole days, the sun shines brightly on the Israelite camp!

After the darkness, Pharaoh summons Moses to the palace. Just a few minutes later Moses returns. "Pharaoh will still not let us go," he says. "But I've spoken with the Lord. It's now time for the final miracle that will convince him to set us free."

Moses asks you to help assemble the Israelite elders. When they're gathered around him, they listen eagerly to his instructions. He tells them that at midnight God will pass through the land and cause the first-born in every house to die. "In order to be spared," Moses explains, "each Israelite family must sacrifice a lamb and sprinkle its blood above the door of their house as a sign to the Lord that they are his people. God also says that each family should roast the lamb and eat it with special bread, made without yeast to save time. Your families should eat standing up, with their coats and shoes on, ready to leave in a hurry."

The elders jump up and rush off to tell the rest of the people. Hours later it begins to grow dark. All the Israelites have made their preparations according to Moses' instructions. Just after midnight, you hear the screams of Egyptians echoing throughout the city as they realize what's happening. Without warning, Pharaoh's guards appear and summon Moses to the palace. You follow hurriedly behind. When you enter the palace, Pharaoh rushes up to Moses. His face is red and his eyes are wide and wet with tears. Pharaoh's own son is dead….

"Leave! Take your people and their livestock and go worship your God!" Pharaoh cries.

You follow as Moses rushes from the palace and begins calling the people to gather their belongings and prepare to leave. Soon the Israelite camp is a bustling caravan of families, wagons, and livestock. They are ready to set off for the land God has promised to give them. You're thrilled that at last the time has arrived for Moses to lead the Israelites out of Egypt. But you're also worried. Pharaoh has changed his mind many times in the past. You wonder if it might happen again. *Maybe I should stay behind in case Pharaoh does change his mind and tries to stop the Israelites,* you think. *Then I can try to warn Moses.* On the other hand, staying in Egypt could be dangerous, and you're not sure you really want to leave Moses and miss this great moment.

If you stay behind, turn to page 49.

If you go with Moses, turn to page 54.

You'd like to go with Moses, but someone should stay behind to warn Moses if Pharaoh changes his mind. You make your way through the crowd of Israelites preparing to leave Egypt and slip back to the palace. Afraid that you might be recognized as an Israelite, you hide behind a nearby wagon. It's been a very long night, and in a moment, you're fast asleep....

Early the next morning you're awakened by the shouts of Pharaoh's guards commanding all men to assemble at the palace. No one can see you, so you sit silently and listen. When the streets have filled with all the men who survived the night, you hear Pharaoh's voice.

"It was a mistake to let the Israelites go!" he yells to the crowd. "All of you who are soldiers must prepare your chariots immediately. We're going after them!"

You were right! Now you must warn Moses as soon as possible! From your hiding place you can see that the gathered crowd is large. *Maybe I can get away without being noticed,* you think. *But what if I'm recognized as an Israelite? It might be better to stay here until the crowd breaks up.*

If you leave your hiding place at once, turn to page 51.

If you stay in your hiding place until the crowd leaves, turn to page 52.

Though you know that you may be recognized, you decide to take the risk. Cautiously you crawl out from beneath the wagon and inch along the back of the crowd. Drawing your cloak over your head, you keep your eyes lowered. When you reach the edge of the crowd, you begin to walk faster. All at once you feel a strong hand grasp you from behind.

"What's the hurry, friend?" asks a gruff voice. "Aren't you interested in what Pharaoh has to say?"

As your eyes meet those of the Egyptian guard, you desperately hope he doesn't recognize you as a friend of Moses. But that hope immediately vanishes. Announcing that he's captured an Israelite, the guard pushes you toward the palace courtyard. Though you think about trying to escape, you realize it's useless. You're already imagining your future as an Egyptian slave. But your heart is at peace. You did what you could to help Moses and your people reach the freedom God has prepared for them.

The End

You breathe slowly and quietly, not moving a muscle, until Pharaoh finishes his speech with a rousing cry. The men shout back in agreement and rush off to prepare for the chase. As soon as the crowd has cleared, you crawl out from behind the wagon, pull your cloak up around your face, and hurry off through the city.

Everywhere men are hitching large, powerful horses to waiting chariots. Just as you're wondering how you're ever going to get to Moses before they do, you see the answer before you. A soldier who has just finished readying his chariot rushes back into his house, leaving the chariot unattended. There's no time to think. You jump onto the chariot, grab the reins, and thunder down the street in an explosion of speed. Because there's so much commotion, you're able to make it out of the city without being stopped. Soon you're frantically racing toward the desert.

While you're wildly urging the horses on, you begin to realize that you have no idea which route Moses has taken! Just as you're starting to panic, you see a huge pillar of cloud towering in the distance. You understand that God must be using the cloud to show Moses the way! You spur the horses on toward the cloud, and soon you can make out the vast crowd of Israelites up ahead. By the time you reach the people, they're beginning to set up camp. Several of the men on the outskirts of the crowd recognize you and shout their welcome. They instantly direct you to Moses. When you finally reach Moses at the front of the camp, you see why the Israelites have stopped. Just on the other side of the camp are the stormy waters of the Red Sea!

"Moses!" you shout. "Pharaoh is coming after you with his army and six hundred chariots!"

"Thank you my friend!" he exclaims. "How bravely you've acted!"

Before you can ask Moses what he's going to do, a group of men come running up behind you.

Turn to page 57.

Although you have your doubts about Pharaoh keeping his word, you decide that you don't want to leave Moses. You follow Moses and Aaron to the front of the throng of people. Moses climbs onto a wagon and prepares to speak to the crowd.

"Children of Israel!" he shouts. "It's time to return to your homeland!"

With that the people let out a loud cheer, and the journey begins. As the gigantic caravan moves away from the city, you look back. What you see in the dim light of early morning amazes you. All around you, as far as you can observe in every direction, are people, wagons, and livestock. You're suddenly aware of just how incredible an exodus this is—there are over a half million Israelites leaving Egypt!

"We must not take the main road," Moses cautions. "There will be Egyptian outposts."

"Look!" shouts Aaron, pointing to the horizon. Before you is a huge cloud in the shape of a pillar, which looks as if it rises out of the ground and reaches all the way to heaven.

"It's the Lord showing us the way to follow!" exclaims Moses.

The journey is especially difficult because you must travel over rough terrain to avoid the Egyptian outposts. When you feel yourself getting tired,

you look up at the pillar of cloud and gain new strength from the knowledge that God is with you. As the sun is beginning to set, you catch sight of the glistening waters of the Red Sea in the distance. You reach the shore just as the sun sinks below the horizon.

"We'll camp here tonight," says Moses.

While you begin to help set up camp, you hear a faint rumble. Then a murmur buzzes through the camp. Some men dash up to Moses. "Pharaoh and his chariots are coming!" they shout in panic. "His whole army is chasing us!"

Turn to page 57.

"Have you brought us out of Egypt only to die?" a voice shrieks from the darkness. "It was better to serve the Egyptians than to perish here in the wilderness!"

"Don't be afraid!" cries Moses. "Stay calm, for the Lord shall fight for you!"

At once, the pillar of cloud begins to shift, as though it's being blown by a great wind. It moves all the way around the Israelite camp to the other side, positioning itself between the Egyptians and the Israelites. Surprisingly, the cloud, which up until this point has remained as bright as fire all during the night, now becomes dark on the side facing the Egyptians. You turn your attention from the cloud to Moses and see that he is walking over to a large stone by the edge of the sea. He climbs up onto the stone, pauses for a moment, then stretches his hands and his staff out over the water. At that moment, a strong east wind begins to blow. It quickly becomes so forceful that your eyes sting. You struggle to watch what's happening. You see the waves growing higher and higher. As the wind continues to howl, you're astonished to see that the water is separating…. You can actually see a dry path in the middle of the water! The sea has parted to make a passageway!

"Quickly! Let's get across!" shouts Moses when the path is complete.

With that the Israelites, all their wagons and livestock, set off through the passage. You stay at the shore with Moses and Aaron, guiding the people into the passageway through the Red Sea. Finally, when the last Israelite has entered the passage, you follow. You feel as if you're dreaming as the wind continues to hold back the sea, forming walls of water on either side of you. When you're about halfway across, you hear a thundering sound behind you. Looking back, you're horrified to see that the Egyptian army has reached the shore and is now entering the passageway!

"Moses!" you scream, "the Egyptians are gaining on us!"

"Yes," Moses replies, with a strange calm.

By the time you've finally reached the shore ahead, the Egyptian army is so close that you can hear the crack of the soldiers' whips as they urge their horses on. With so many people and young children, as well as livestock, the Israelites can't possibly outrun Pharaoh's army! But then you notice that the Egyptian chariots are slowing down. The soldiers are having trouble with their chariot wheels. They also seem to be very frightened. Facing the water, Moses again raises his hand over the sea. You watch in wonder as the walls of water come crashing down on the Egyptians with a deafening roar. Within seconds, the passageway disappears and the water flows back to its normal depth.

On the shore, the throng of Israelites breaks into a loud cheer. Moses turns toward the crowd, his eyes sparkling with the joy of triumph. "We must celebrate in the Lord's honor," he shouts above their voices.

All the people break into hymns of praise, which echo across the waters of the Red Sea. Moses' sister Miriam comes forward with a tambourine. Other women come dancing behind her. Miriam sings loudly:

> "Sing to the Lord, for he has triumphed gloriously!

> "He has thrown the horses and their riders into the sea!"

The celebration continues all day and into the evening, with a feast and singing of the Lord's praises.

Turn to page 60.

The first thing the next morning you follow Moses to the head of the caravan as he leads the Israelites on the next leg of their journey. While you're happy about the victory over the Egyptians, you realize that a long and dangerous trip through the desert still lies ahead of you.

As you move through the rough terrain, you often stop to help people who find the sweltering heat especially unbearable. With the wagons and all the livestock, travel is hard work, and the caravan moves slowly. By the third day, the water supply is beginning to run low and the people are becoming restless with worry. Around sunset, a few men in the lead shout that they see water and run toward a stream. But when they taste the water, they spit it out immediately. "It's bitter!" they cry to Moses. "What shall we do?"

Moses prays and receives an answer from the Lord. You watch as Moses steps up to the stream and throws a piece of wood into the water. "Take another drink," he tells the men.

They slowly approach the water, drink a sip from their hands, and turn in amazement toward the crowd. "It's sweet now!" they exclaim. "We can drink it!"

Excitedly you join your thirsty fellow travelers for a drink before setting up camp for the night.

At the first streak of dawn, you're up again. Your muscles ache from the rigors of traveling, but you help those around you take down their tents and pack their wagons.

After another long day in the desert, you again hear shouting at the front of the caravan. Edging your way up, you can hardly believe your eyes. Before you stands a beautiful green oasis—complete with fresh springs of water and tall palm trees!

"This is Elim," says Moses. "We'll camp here tonight."

Everyone gets to work setting up camp under the cool shade of the trees. In spite of the peacefulness of Elim, you sense that some of the people are again becoming very restless. During your meal, some men start talking about life back in Egypt. "At least we always had plenty of food and water there," one declares.

"And even though the work was hard, it was nothing like traveling through this wasteland of a desert!" another breaks in.

"Is there far to go?" one of the men asks you.

"Yes," you say, remembering your early travels. "It's a very long journey."

At daybreak, Moses has the horns sounded to wake the camp. You notice that everyone is slower to get up, and you hear many people complaining about having to leave the beautiful oasis for the wilderness ahead. By the midmorning the sun's rays are scorching. It seems hotter than it's ever been. Around noon, the men you were talking to the night before approach you.

"We don't want to go on," says one. "We're already running low on food and water, and there's nothing but barren land ahead of us. Our life in Egypt was better. We want to go back. Will you come with us?"

You pause for a moment. There *is* a long journey ahead, and it *won't* be easy traveling with a half million people. Maybe the men are right. But how could you abandon your friend Moses? Maybe you should have more faith in the Lord to see you through this difficult journey.

If you go with the men back to Egypt, turn to page 63.

If you stay with Moses and the Israelites, turn to page 65.

"You're right," you tell the men. "Life in Egypt is better than suffering in the desert without food and water."

You turn to look for Moses, but one of the men stops you. "We must not waste another minute," he says. "Let's go!"

Although you feel bad about leaving without saying good-bye to Moses, your desire to get out of the desert is stronger. You follow the men back through the crowd to the rear of the caravan. When you tell the people what you're doing, they just shake their heads and look away.

You set off in the direction of Egypt. You're able to make such progress that soon the Israelites are just a speck on the horizon behind you. Before long you reach Elim, where you spend a relaxing evening resting under the palm trees and talking about the journey ahead.

The next day you're up early, feeling refreshed. Because you're such a small group, you're again able to travel very swiftly. Soon enough, you find yourself at the shore of the Red Sea. This makes you think back to the miracle of the parting of the waters that God worked through Moses. You realize how much you miss Moses. But it's too late to turn back.

"We can use this to cross over," says one of the men, pointing to a small wooden boat on the shore.

You're nervous, because you're not a strong swimmer. But you have no choice. It's crowded in the boat, yet you all manage to squeeze in. The sea is smooth, and the rowing is easy. Then, without warning, a wind begins to blow in from the shore. The sun hides behind dark clouds as the wind picks up. The water is so choppy now it's impossible to keep rowing. Waves are washing over you. A huge one suddenly slams into the boat, flipping it upside down! You're all thrown into the water. As you struggle to keep afloat, you wish you were back in the desert again…with Moses.

The End

"I believe that God will take care of us on this journey," you tell the men. "And I don't want to leave my friend Moses. Why don't you stay with us? Let's pray to God. He'll help us. He'll give us strength."

But the men won't listen. They turn away and head back toward Egypt.

Your decision to stay with Moses gives you strength for the rest of the long day's journey. But many people are still grumbling. You search for Moses to tell him about this, but as you approach him, you see a group of men already there complaining.

"It would have been better to die in Egypt as slaves with plenty of food," shrieks one of the men, "than to starve to death out here in the wilderness!"

Moses looks troubled, and doesn't answer for several minutes. "The Lord has told me," he finally says, "that he will provide for us. He will send us meat in the evening and bread in the morning. You must have faith."

The men return to their families and you move on in the desert heat. Soon the sky is the brilliant orange of sunset, and it's time to pitch your tents for the night. Your stomach growls with hunger as you work. All at once, as though dropped from heaven, the sky is filled with quail! The birds land

all over the camp and the hungry people scramble to catch them. That night you enjoy the best meal you've had in weeks as the whole camp feasts on quail. You fall asleep feeling very satisfied.

When the rising horns sound the next morning, you get up and glance outside your tent. You can hardly believe your eyes—the ground is all white! Could it be frost? You look around and see Moses smiling broadly.

"This is the bread that God has given us to eat!" he shouts to the people.

You join the others in gathering this bread, which the Israelites call manna. It tastes very good, like a sweet wafer.

"Gather only a day's supply," Moses tells the people as they continue to collect the manna. "If anyone gathers more than that, it will spoil. Only on the sixth day may you take more, so that you can rest and worship God on the seventh day."

When everyone has enough manna for the day, you pack up camp and again set off through the desert. The journey is as difficult as ever, but the provisions from God have given everyone extra energy. You travel along for days through the wilderness, always having plenty to eat because the manna appears every morning. But there has been no sign of water, and the supply for the entire caravan begins to run low. Once again some of the Israelites begin to talk about life back in Egypt. One night, as you're camped in a place called Rephidim, a group approaches Moses.

"Now we have no water," they say. "Have you brought us here to die of thirst?"

Moses looks worried and walks off by himself to speak with the Lord. When he returns, he asks you to summon the Israelite elders. You rush through the camp and soon return with as many of the elders as you could find. Moses goes before the people and the elders with his staff in hand. He approaches a huge rock and hits it with his staff. As you watch in awe, water begins pouring out of the rock!

"When will you learn not to doubt that God is with us?" Moses asks the elders.

You spend that evening and the following morning distributing water throughout the camp. That afternoon, as you're resting and talking with Moses, a young Israelite struggling to catch his breath comes running up.

"There's a tribe gathering just outside the camp!" he reports frantically.

"It's the Amalekites," responds Moses. "We must hurry to defend ourselves!"

You've heard stories about this wandering tribe, disturbing stories about its occasional attacks on travelers.

Moses summons Joshua, one of the younger leaders of the Israelites, and tells him to raise an army to fight the Amalekites. "During the battle I will be standing on the top of the hill holding the staff of God in my hand," Moses promises.

Joshua nods. Before he hurries back to the camp, he turns to you.

"I've watched you serve as a leader in the caravan," he says, "and I know what a trusted friend you are to Moses. I'd be honored if you'd join my army to fight the Amalekites."

You're flattered by Joshua's offer, but you know that it's very dangerous to oppose such powerful warriors. You want to continue to help your friend Moses. You wonder if it might be better to stay at his side rather than risk your life in battle.

If you accept Joshua's offer, turn to page 70.

If you stay in the camp with Moses, turn to page 72.

"I'd be honored to join your army," you answer
Joshua.

"I worry for your safety," Moses breaks in, "for
the Amalekites are fierce warriors. But I'm proud
that you want to fight for the Lord and your
people."

Moses embraces you and you set off with
Joshua. You help him go through the camp calling
for volunteers to defend your people against the
Amalekites. Many men step forward, and soon
Joshua has assembled a large army.

The next day, the Israelite army stands opposite the Amalekites in the desert. The enemies'
swords gleam in the sun as they prepare to charge.
You feel afraid, but then glancing to your right,
you see Moses standing on a hill. He's holding the
staff he's used to work so many miracles high in
the air. This fills you with confidence as the warriors begin to charge.

"Let's go out to meet them!" shouts Joshua.

The army follows Joshua's lead and rushes toward the Amalekites. At once you find yourself in
the middle of a fierce battle. All around, you hear
swords clashing and men screaming as you struggle
to hold off the enemy. The Amalekites seem bigger and stronger than your men. In no time your
arms are so tired that it's a struggle even to hold

up your sword. You try to get behind your lines for a rest, but you're surrounded by Amalekites. Then something flashes directly to your left. Your shoulder explodes with pain and you fall to the ground. As you look up at the Amalekite holding his sword over you, you don't regret having sacrificed your life so that your people may continue on the journey to the Promised Land. Because of your faith in God, you know that this is not the end, but a new and wonderful beginning.

The End

"Thank you," you say to Joshua, "but I think I should stay with Moses."

"He's very fortunate to have a friend like you," Joshua replies before rushing off to begin assembling his army.

Moses tells you how happy he is that you've decided to stay with him, and he asks you to come with him to watch the battle.

Before long Joshua gathers a large group of soldiers and leads them out into the desert to face the Amalekites. You go with Moses to a hill from which you can view the entire battlefield. As they are about to meet the enemy, Joshua and his army look up at Moses. Moses takes his staff and raises it high into the air. This seems to give the Israelites courage and energy. At first they're able to fight off the fierce warriors, but as the battle continues, the Amalekites appear to be gaining ground on Joshua and his army. Glancing over at Moses, you see that his arms have grown so tired, he can no longer hold up his staff.

"We must help Moses hold the staff up!" shouts Hur, one of the Israelite leaders who has come to watch the battle.

Hur motions for you and Aaron to go over to a large rock a few feet away. The three of you roll the rock to Moses so that he can sit down. Hur and Aaron then stand on either side of Moses and hold his arms up. As soon as his arms are raised, you look down at the battlefield. You can sense the new strength that's surging through the Israelites. Soon they've pushed the Amalekites so far back, that the enemy warriors turn and run for the hills. Joshua's army lets out a loud cheer and returns to the camp for a victory celebration.

The next day, it's time to continue the journey to the land God has promised your people. Again the horns sound at dawn, and you help pack up the camp. After a few more days of travel, the terrain begins to look very familiar. After some time you realize that you're back in the area of Midian. In the distance you can see the mountain where your adventure began.

"Moses!" you say excitedly, "there's Mount Sinai, where we used to tend sheep."

"Yes," he replies. "God has instructed me to camp there."

When the camp is set up, you and Moses sit, gazing up at the mountain and reminiscing about your days as shepherds. As you're talking, a young Israelite approaches. "Excuse me, Moses," he says shyly. "There is someone here to see you."

You look beyond the young man and see that it's Jethro.

"Ah, my father-in-law!" Moses cries out, breaking into a wide smile. "How wonderful to see you!"

You both embrace Jethro and ask about life in Midian. He tells you how happy and peaceful his life has been, and you again think back to the days you spent working for him. After some minutes of conversation, Moses is called away to help resolve a dispute between some men in the camp.

"Does he do this often?" Jethro asks you.

"Yes," you answer. "Since our journey began, Moses has spent a lot of time giving advice in the name of God. There's always some matter needing his attention."

It's almost an hour before Moses returns. When he does, Jethro tells Moses that it's not good for him to spend so much time and energy settling all the people's disagreements. "Why don't you choose some trustworthy men and assign them to make decisions in ordinary cases?" Jethro suggests. "That way you won't be under so much pressure, and you can save your energy for more important matters."

Moses nods in agreement. "Thank you for your wise advice, Jethro," he gratefully replies, before going off to tell the elders of his plan.

"My friend," Jethro says turning to you, "I have an offer for you. I could really use help in the fields, and since you were one of the best shepherds I've ever had, I'd like you to come back to Midian and work for me."

Being near Midian again has reminded you of the happy years you spent there. It would be wonderful to return to such a peaceful life after all you've been through. But you've come so far with Moses. You're not sure you want to leave him before he reaches the Promised Land.

If you go with Jethro, turn to page 76.

If you stay with Moses and continue the journey, turn to page 21.

You don't want to leave Moses, but the opportunity to peacefully live out your life as a shepherd is too tempting to pass up. When you tell Moses of your decision, he's disappointed but understanding and he wishes you well.

You say good-bye to the many friends you've made on the journey, then return to Midian with Jethro. As you settle back into your life as a shepherd, you admit that you miss Moses terribly. You tell yourself that you'll get over it. But you don't. As time goes on, you find yourself thinking more and more often of your friend. You begin to regret your decision to return to Midian. You begin seeking out travelers and asking them for any news of Moses and the Israelites in the land of Canaan. One day, as you're speaking with some travelers by the side of the road, a man approaches you.

"I heard you mention Canaan," he says. "That's where we're headed. Would you like to join us?"

You're so excited at the thought of seeing Moses again that you say yes without even thinking it over. The man waits while you rush back to say good-bye to Jethro and collect your belongings. When you return, he invites you to ride in his wagon for the first part of the trip. You climb in and set off on the journey. After about an hour, the wagon abruptly stops. The man jumps into the back with you. Two other men follow.

"I'd like you to meet my friends," the first man snickers, as another begins to rummage through your belongings.

"Wait!" you say. "Those are mine!"

"Not anymore," snarls the second thief.

You try to grab your bag, but one of the men throws you off the wagon. As it hurriedly pulls away, you pray that a friendly caravan will come along soon. That will be your only hope of making it to Canaan and joining Moses…

The End

After Jethro returns to Midian, Moses goes high up the mountain. When he returns after several hours, he calls for you. "Help me to spread this message throughout the camp," he says. "We have two days to clean our tents and our clothes because God is going to appear to us on the third day."

After delivering this exciting message to the people, you spend the next two days washing all your clothes and cleaning the area around the front of the camp where you live with Moses, Aaron, and the Israelite elders.

On the morning of the third day, splitting peals of thunder wake you. The force of the thunder is so great that the ground beneath you seems to be trembling. You stumble out of the tent and stare up at the mountain. Clouds as dark as night completely hide its peak, while bolts of lightning flash across the sky. Between cracks of thunder, you hear trumpets blaring. You nervously scan the camp. All of the Israelites—pale and fearful—stand with their eyes fixed on the mountain. Turning back to it yourself, you catch sight of Moses standing on a huge rock at its base. The thunder dies down for a moment.

"Don't come near the mountain!" Moses shouts to the people before heading up to the peak himself. He disappears into the thick clouds. As soon as he's gone, the thunder returns. The ground is shaking so violently that it's hard to keep your balance. Lightning continues to streak the menacing sky, and a strong wind howls across the camp. Some of the Israelites scream in fear, while others remain speechless at this astonishing display of God's power. After some time you see Moses coming down from the mountain through the clouds.

"Speak to us, and we will listen," cries one of the elders to Moses. "But don't let God speak to us, for we might die!"

"Don't be afraid!" Moses replies. "God has come to test you. He wants you only to be afraid of sinning against him."

With these few words spoken, Moses turns and climbs back up the mountain to continue talking to God. Gradually the thunder and lightning fade, and the people gather in groups. They talk about the glory of God that they've seen. Later that day Aaron approaches you.

"Moses has told us to gather the elders," he says. "Since the people have agreed to live by his law, there will be a sacrificial feast to honor the Lord."

You help Aaron gather the elders, and not long after you find yourself at a table with Moses at the head. He speaks of the laws that the Lord has given, most important of which are the Ten Commandments:

I am the Lord your God:

You shall not have other gods besides me.

You shall not take the name of the Lord your God in vain.

Remember to keep holy the Lord's day.

Honor your father and your mother.

You shall not kill.

You shall not commit adultery.

You shall not steal.

You shall not bear false witness against your neighbor.

You shall not covet your neighbor's wife.

You shall not covet your neighbor's goods.

Moses describes the other laws that God has given him. Then he asks if the elders, as representatives of the Israelites, agree to obey these laws. Everyone at the table says yes, and the agreement is sealed with a sacrifice. After the meal, Moses stands to address the entire gathering.

"It's time for me to go back up the mountain," he says, "to hear the rest of God's instructions for us. Wait for me."

Joshua leads Moses to the mountain, and you return with Aaron and the others to the camp. There the Israelites are still talking about the wonderful show of God's power and glory.

As time goes on things settle down and the people return to the daily routine of life in the camp. Still, no one goes near the mountain.

Days stretch into weeks and Moses has still not come down from the mountain. Some of the Israelites begin to get worried.

"Where is Moses?" a group of men asks Aaron one day. "We don't know what's happened to him. Maybe he's dead. Make a god for us to worship, so that we might have a feast for the Lord."

Aaron instructs the men to gather gold jewelry from which he can make a god to worship. He then turns to you.

"Will you help me?" he asks.

You hesitate. You want to help Aaron, but you remember God's instructions not to have any other gods besides him and not to worship any graven images. *Maybe it would be better to wait for Moses and not take part in this.*

If you help Aaron, turn to page 83.

If you wait for Moses, turn to page 85.

"Yes, I'll help," you tell Aaron.

You go around the camp gathering gold jewelry and bring it back to Aaron. He melts the gold down and molds it into a statue in the shape of a calf, which he sets up in the middle of the camp. He then announces that there will be a feast for the Lord around the golden calf.

Soon many people are dancing before this golden calf and singing the praises of God. While this seems strange to you, a few Israelites explain that this is the way people worshipped in Egypt. That makes sense to you, so you join in the singing and dancing. After a few minutes the celebration is interrupted by a crashing sound from the mountain above. You look up to see Moses, his face red with anger, shattering slabs of stone on the rocks at his feet.

"What's this?!" he screams. "You will be punished for breaking the Lord's Commandments!"

You want to approach Moses and try to explain, but he's busy giving instructions to a group of men. Before you have a chance, these men draw their swords and charge toward you and the others who were dancing around the golden calf. You try to run, but there's no escape. You realize that it was wrong not to obey God's command...

The End

You tell Aaron that you don't think it's a good idea to create a god to worship, and you walk away. You watch from a distance as Aaron collects gold jewelry, melts it down, and molds a golden calf. He puts it in the middle of the camp, and some of the Israelites begin to sing and dance around it. As you watch the people worship the golden calf, you hear something behind you. You turn to see Joshua leading Moses down the mountain. Moses' eyes are ablaze with anger when he sees what's happening. He throws down the stone tablets he's carrying and charges into the camp, shouting for Aaron.

"Why did you let the people do this?" he demands.

Aaron tries to explain, but Moses calls for those loyal to the Lord to come forward. He commands a group of men to punish those who worshipped the golden calf, and you watch as they slay those who were dancing around the statue.

The next day, Moses is not as angry, and he goes back up the mountain to ask the Lord to forgive the people. This time, all the people wait patiently, and soon Moses appears above the camp. His entire face seems to glow with the glory of God, and he's holding two stone slabs upon which are written the Ten Commandments.

"These are the words that the Lord has commanded!" he shouts.

When Moses returns to the camp, he says that there is much work to be done. "God has given me instructions to build a portable dwelling in which we will worship him," Moses announces. "The Lord asks all Israelites to make offerings of gold, wood, animal skins, and other materials to help build the dwelling."

You quickly run off to your tent and return with some of your best skins. After you place them on the pile of donations, Moses takes you aside. "I've asked Bezalel and Oholiab to take charge of building the dwelling because they're expert craftsmen," he says. "They've requested some assistants to help with the work and to care for the dwelling on the journey to the Promised Land. I thought of you."

It sounds like a wonderful challenge. *It could be very rewarding to be involved in the building of God's place of worship,* you think. *But it will mean seeing less of Moses...*

If you help build the dwelling, turn to page 87.

If you stay with Moses, turn to page 90.

"I'd consider it an honor to help build the Lord's dwelling!" you tell Moses.

He leads you over to a field at the edge of the camp, where Bezalel and Oholiab have already started building according to the instructions Moses has received from God. They welcome you and get you started in your work immediately. It's very hard labor, especially with the desert sun beating down on you, but you feel enthused when you think of the important job you're doing for God.

First you put up a large wooden frame, which you cover with curtains of linen, mohair cloth, and animal skins. Inside are two rooms. One has an altar with a golden candlestick and twelve loaves of bread—a loaf for each of the tribes of Israel. The other room, called the Most Holy Place, is very special. In this room is a wooden chest called the ark. The tablets upon which the Ten Commandments are written will be stored in the ark, along with Moses' staff and a pot of manna, the bread from heaven.

It takes many weeks of hard work, but finally your small group of workers finishes the dwelling.

"Thank you for your help, my friend," Moses says to you, as he looks it over. "This is a very special place."

The next day Moses calls all the people to gather in the field before the dwelling. Aaron and his sons, in their colorful priests' robes, come forward to lead the first service in the new place of worship. As you beam with pride at the sight of the holy place you helped to build, the cloud, which had been hanging over the mountain, begins to move across the sky, settling right over the dwelling. God is showing his approval of your work!

Not long after the first service in the dwelling, the cloud slowly moves out over the desert. You know it's time to continue on your journey.

The family of Levi is appointed to look after the dwelling, and Moses asks you to be their special assistant. This is almost as difficult a job as building the dwelling was, since you must take the dwelling apart, store all the materials, and rebuild it at the next stop. Even though it's not easy, you feel privileged to help with this work. Caring for the dwelling keeps you so busy that you don't even notice how long the rest of the journey is.

Soon enough you reached the border of the Promised Land. But scouting parties discover that there is a strong tribe living there. While Joshua wants to try to defeat the tribe immediately, confident that God is on your side, many Israelites are afraid and again wish they were back in Egypt. This angers the Lord, and Moses must once more plead with God to forgive the Israelites.

"God will not strike you," Moses says to the people, "but you will not enter the Promised Land. You will wander in the wilderness for the rest of your lives, then your children will enter the land with the Lord's blessing."

This news saddens everyone in the camp, including you. After the long, hard journey from Egypt you are now faced with more years of wandering. One day, when you're feeling discouraged, you go to talk to Moses.

"There's no reason to feel sad," he tells you. "You've had a wonderful life serving the Lord. Now you must try to have more faith in God and accept his plans. They're always for our good."

You take Moses' words to heart as you live out your life in the wilderness. Every day you're up at dawn. You're kept busy taking care of the dwelling. Looking after God's place of worship fills you with a special kind of peace. You spend many hours with your friend Moses, talking about all you've been through together and looking forward to being together with God in heaven...

The End

You thank Moses for the offer, but tell him that you'd rather stay at his side for the journey to the Promised Land.

"Yes, I understand," he says. "I'm always happy to have you near me."

Over the next several weeks you accompany Moses every day to check on the progress of the dwelling. When it's finally finished, Moses calls for the entire camp to gather around the dwelling for the first service. Aaron and his sons, wearing bright, colorful robes, lead the service. The sight of the beautiful new dwelling, with its beautiful curtains and gold trim, and all of God's people worshipping before it under the desert sun takes your breath away. Suddenly a shadow moves across the crowd. You look up to see the cloud, which has been hanging over the mountain where Moses talked to God. It positions itself over the dwelling, and you smile at God's way of showing his approval.

When you get up the next day, you go outside to take another look at the dwelling. You notice that the cloud has left it and is now moving ahead. You run and tell Moses. He nods. "It's time to continue on," he says.

Moses sends out orders to pack up camp and prepare to resume the journey. Soon you find yourself back on the road, at Moses' side at the head of the caravan. For the first few days the weather is beautiful and you and Moses talk excitedly of how close the Promised Land seems. But the people start to complain again about how difficult the journey is. One after another, they come up to tell Moses how tired they are of walking or how much they miss their lives in Egypt. You're amazed at how patiently Moses handles the different problems, as he continues to seek guidance from the Lord and always manages to keep the caravan moving.

"We're now very close to the land God has promised us," he says to you one sunny day.

"This is wonderful!" you reply.

"But we're not there yet," he cautions with a smile. "We must still find out about the kind of people who live there."

That evening Moses calls together leaders from the twelve tribes of Israel and gives them instructions to go out and scout the land and its people. One of these leaders is Joshua, who led the victory over the Amalekites. After the meeting, Joshua comes to you.

"I know that you're a good friend of Moses," he says, "and I value your judgment. I'd like you to come with me as an assistant on this scouting mission."

The thought of going on a mission to explore this new land is exciting, but it could be dangerous. You ask Moses what he thinks. "I'd rather have you stay with me in the camp, but I'll respect your decision," he answers.

If you go on the scouting mission, turn to page 93.

If you stay with Moses, turn to page 97.

You inform Joshua and Moses of your decision and rush off to get ready. Soon you're back at the head of the camp, ready to set off with Joshua, the other Israelite leaders, and their assistants.

"God be with you," says Moses. "We'll be praying for you."

Your group makes its way over the green hills and into the land beyond. That night you camp in a grove of trees beside a stream. You get up at daybreak and travel further into the interior of the territory. By afternoon you find yourself in a lush valley, with trees bearing many fruits you've never seen before.

"This is a wonderful land!" you exclaim to Joshua as you collect samples of the fruits you find.

"Yes," he agrees. "But we have yet to see the people."

You move on further, continuing to find the land rich and abundant. At one point some of the other scouts find a cluster of grapes so big that they have to carry it on a pole between them. Eventually, as you round a hill, you spot settlements down below. You and Joshua steal down to get a closer look. You approach a small house surrounded by a garden. By the side of the house you see several baskets filled with huge pomegranates.

"We're supposed to bring back fruit," you remind Joshua. "Should I go get some?"

"No," Joshua replies, "it's too dangerous. There are probably men in the house. We need to be very careful."

You agree that you must be cautious, but it really doesn't look like anyone is home.

If you ignore Joshua's advice and try to get some fruit, turn to page 95.

If you stay back with Joshua, turn to page 96.

You feel a little guilty about ignoring Joshua's advice, but you're sure you can make it to the house and back very quickly. You run off before he can stop you. As you get closer, you see several spears, a bow, and a quiver of arrows leaning against a wall of the house. This makes you very uneasy, but you've almost reached the fruit, so you decide to keep going. As you near a basket, you accidentally knock over a spear.

"What was that?" a deep voice bellows from within the house.

You quickly snatch a pomegranate and begin running as fast as you can back toward Joshua. A door slams behind you. There's a rustling outside the house followed by a loud twang. An arrow whizzes past your ear. You try to run faster, but the grove where Joshua is hiding is still several feet ahead. Suddenly a strong hand clutches your arm.

"A new slave!" the deep voice booms.

If only I'd listened to Joshua! you think as the man leads you back to the house.

The End

"You're right," you answer Joshua. "Look at those spears and arrows leaning against the wall."

"These people are probably very powerful," Joshua replies. "But I'm sure we can defeat them with God's help."

You nod in agreement and follow as Joshua makes his way back through the woods away from the house. After several more hours of exploring the land, you meet up with the other scouts, and return to tell the Israelites of what you've discovered. When you walk back into the camp, exhausted from the mission, the people give you a hero's welcome. Moses and the elders rush up, anxious to hear all about your discoveries.

Turn to page 98.

"I'd rather stay here," you say. "My days of exploration are over."

Joshua nods and rushes off to prepare for the scouting mission. Soon he has all the leaders assembled. After Moses says a prayer for them, the scouts set off over the green hills beyond the camp. During the next few days, time seems to pass very slowly. Everyone in the camp is very anxious to hear about the Promised Land.

Finally, one afternoon, you see the group of scouts approaching in the distance. Word spreads quickly through the camp, and by the time they arrive there's an anxious crowd waiting.

"What did you find?" shout the Israelites.

Turn to page 98.

"The land is very rich and abundant," says one of the leaders. "Look at the fruit we've brought back."

You can hear many people in the crowd gasping in awe as samples of the different fruits are held up.

"What about the people?" someone yells.

Another scout steps forward. "The people are very powerful and live in great walled cities."

"But," assures Caleb, Joshua's friend and fellow scout, "we can defeat them with God on our side. Let's go now and take this land!"

Joshua moves over to stand with Caleb and shows his support, but you see that the other scouts are not as sure.

"No, no!" cries one of them. "The men there are giants who make us look like tiny grasshoppers. We'll never defeat them!"

A murmur runs through the crowd, and you can see fear on the faces of those standing closest to you. Voices grow louder and several men push their way to the front.

"It would have been better to die in Egypt!" they scream. "The Lord has brought us all this way just to be killed. Let's return to Egypt!"

"No!" shouts Joshua, standing with Caleb, as Moses and Aaron bow in prayer behind them.

"This is a good land, and we must have faith in the Lord to bring us into it."

By now the crowd is wild with fear. Many people are yelling and arguing with Joshua and Caleb. Suddenly a rock streaks through the air, just barely missing Joshua's head. Another rock follows, striking Caleb on the shoulder. *If the people are so afraid that they're actually throwing rocks at Joshua and Caleb, maybe they're right,* you think. *Maybe I should join them in the hope of making it back to Egypt.* But you think of how good a friend Joshua is to you and Moses, and you see how Moses is praying behind him in support. Besides, Joshua still has faith that God *will* bring you to the Promised Land.

If you join the crowd and rebel against Joshua and Caleb, turn to page 101.

If you have faith and go stand with Joshua and Caleb, turn to page 103.

Although you really don't want to abandon Joshua and Moses, you begin to feel that you're all caught in a hopeless situation. You move away from Joshua and into the screaming mass of people. Soon, you too are shouting. When someone thrusts a rock into your hand, you throw it, hitting Joshua on the arm. Suddenly there's a rumbling from the dwelling tent, which is set up nearby. Then the unmistakable voice of God speaking to Moses echoes through the camp. "What must I do for the people to have faith in me?! Perhaps I should destroy them and make of you a new and greater nation!"

Moses rushes forward and begs God to spare the Israelites. The Lord instructs Moses and Aaron to tell the people that those who had no faith in him will not enter the Promised Land. Instead, they will wander in the wilderness and die there. When the people hear this, they again begin to murmur.

"If this is the alternative, then we should go ahead and try to enter the Promised Land!" someone cries.

"Yes!"

"He's right!"

"Let's go!"

People all around you are shouting their agreement. You feel that you have no choice. You decide to join the effort to take over the land of Canaan.

Just after dawn the next day, you find yourself in the midst of the same crowd, ready for your attempt to enter the Promised Land. As the crowd sets off for the hills, you see Moses standing on a rock just to the side.

"You're disobeying the Lord!" he shouts. "God is not with you, and you will be killed!"

Hearing this, your heart begins to pound. But you're now in the middle of a mass of people, which is pushing and surging forward in spite of the warning. It's too late to turn back. The men in the lead yell their commands and the crowd presses on. Soon you're approaching the hills that mark the border of Canaan. When you look up at the ridges to either side of you, your heart sinks. There, shining in the morning sun, are rows and rows of raised arrows and spears! The men of Canaan stand ready to defend their land. Letting out a shrill battle cry, they charge into the valley. You're trapped! You turn and try to run back to Moses, but the panicking crowd knocks you to the ground. You struggle to get to your feet, but it's no use. You close your eyes and pray. *Forgive me Lord, I should have trusted you...*

The End

You fight your way through the hostile crowd to stand beside Joshua and Caleb. You're so close that you have to dodge a few rocks yourself, but you have faith that God will protect you. Without warning the ground begins to rumble beneath you, and a mighty voice echoes from the dwelling tent. It's God speaking to Moses! "What must I do for the people to have faith in me?! Perhaps I should destroy them and make of you a new and greater nation!"

The people freeze in terror as the voice of the Lord echoes across the camp. Moses jumps up and rushes to the tent.

"Please forgive them, Lord," he pleads.

He manages to convince God not to destroy the Israelites, but God decides that those who did not have faith will not be allowed to enter the Promised Land. They will spend the rest of their lives wandering in the surrounding wilderness. Upon hearing this, a group of men decide to try to enter the Promised Land anyway. But the people already living there quickly defeat them.

A few days later, it's again time to pick up camp and set off into the wilderness. For many, many years, the caravan wanders around the desert that surrounds Canaan. It's very difficult to endure after being *so* close to the Promised Land, and many people complain and challenge Moses' leadership. Just as before, Moses is very patient in dealing with the people and their problems. You are always by his side to lend your support. You're proud that Moses has become such a great leader. Under his direction, the children of the Israelites who came from Egypt grow up bold and excited about moving into the Promised Land. Even as you grow old and tired after many years of roaming the desert, speaking with Moses always raises your spirits. One day he comes up to you and rests his hand on your arm.

"The time of wandering will soon be over," he says. "But I will only bring our people to the border. Joshua will lead them into the Promised Land."

You smile at the look of peace on Moses' face. When you're camped at the border, Moses climbs up on a rock before the people to give his farewell speech. His eyes shine as brightly as they did when you first met him in the fields of Midian, and his voice booms over the immense throng. He first reminds the people of the laws that the Lord has set forth for them in the agreement made at Mount Sinai. Then he blesses all the tribes of Israel. Next he calls Joshua forward.

"Be strong and of good courage," he says, laying his hands on Joshua's shoulders, "for you will lead these people into the land God has given you. You shall be happy, Israel, for the Lord is with you!"

Tears well up in your eyes, and as you look around you see that everyone is weeping. Moses steps down from the rock and begins to walk toward Mount Nebo, which towers above the camp. Suddenly he stops and looks back at you. He doesn't need to say a word. His eyes express his love and gratitude for your faithful friendship. He turns away and slowly climbs up the mountain, going at last to rest with the Lord in peace.

The next day, as Joshua gives orders for the Israelites to break up camp and prepare to finally end their long journey, you know that your journey has also ended. As the new generation moves toward their Promised Land, you close your eyes and look forward to your promised land—eternal life in heaven with God and your friend Moses.

The End

BOOKS & MEDIA

The Daughters of St. Paul operate book and media centers at the following addresses. Visit, call or write the one nearest you today, or find us on the World Wide Web, www.pauline.org

California

3908 Sepulveda Blvd., Culver City, CA 90230; 310-397-8676

5945 Balboa Ave., San Diego, CA 92111; 858-565-9181

46 Geary Street, San Francisco, CA 94108; 415-781-5180

Florida

145 S.W. 107th Ave., Miami, FL 33174; 305-559-6715

Hawaii

1143 Bishop Street, Honolulu, HI 96813; 808-521-2731

Neighbor Islands call: 800-259-8463

Illinois

172 North Michigan Ave., Chicago, IL 60601; 312-346-4228

Louisiana

4403 Veterans Memorial Blvd., Metairie, LA 70006; 504-887-7631

Massachusetts

Rte. 1, 885 Providence Hwy., Dedham, MA 02026; 781-326-5385

Missouri

9804 Watson Rd., St. Louis, MO 63126; 314-965-3512

New Jersey

561 U.S. Route 1, Wick Plaza, Edison, NJ 08817; 732-572-1200

New York

150 East 52nd Street, New York, NY 10022; 212-754-1110

78 Fort Place, Staten Island, NY 10301; 718-447-5071

Ohio

2105 Ontario Street, Cleveland, OH 44115; 216-621-9427

Pennsylvania

9171-A Roosevelt Blvd., Philadelphia, PA 19114; 215-676-9494

South Carolina

243 King Street, Charleston, SC 29401; 843-577-0175

Tennessee

4811 Poplar Ave., Memphis, TN 38117; 901-761-2987

Texas

114 Main Plaza, San Antonio, TX 78205; 210-224-8101

Virginia

1025 King Street, Alexandria, VA 22314; 703-549-3806

Canada

3022 Dufferin Street, Toronto, Ontario, Canada M6B 3T5; 416-781-9131

1155 Yonge Street, Toronto, Ontario, Canada M4T 1W2; 416-934-3440

¡También somos su fuente para libros, videos y música en español!